Two Sisters and Some Hornets

by
BERYL EPSTEIN
&
DORRIT DAVIS
pictures by
ROSEMARY WELLS

Holiday House · New York

Two
Sisters
and
Some
Hornets

Two Sisters and Some Hornets

"Watch out, Gertrude! That was a hornet that just flew past you. Horrid things! They always remind me of that time in the outhouse at Aunt Hattie's farm. Do you remember?"

"Of course I remember, Agnes. We city children were used to a proper flush toilet in a real indoor bathroom. Aunt Hattie's outhouse was certainly something new to us."

"I wasn't thinking of the outhouse, Gertrude. I was remembering how I was almost stung to death by the hornets in there.

"I was covered with stings. Aunt Hattie had to cut off all my hair to get the hornets out of it."

"What nonsense, Agnes! You were stung a few times that day. We both were, but you *never* had your hair cut off!"

"I did so, Gertrude, and it was your fault, because you stirred up the hornets by banging the door."

"I did no such thing, Agnes! When Aunt Hattie told us to go to the outhouse before we started home, our little cousin Morty said, 'Sometimes there are hornets in there, but I'll scare them away for you.' And he ran ahead and banged the door hard, three or four times. Of course he didn't know he was just stirring the hornets up."

"Well maybe you didn't actually bang the door, Gertrude, but you did keep me shut up in there while the hornets attacked me. Zzzz-zzzzzzz-zzz! Oh, I can hear them now. 'Let me out,' I begged you. 'Please, Gertrude!' But you wouldn't."

"Agnes, you don't really remember what happened that day because you were too young. But I remember perfectly. Everything was quiet when we first went into the outhouse and I began to unbutton your panties for you. You were so pokey learning to do them yourself."

"Gertrude, I never even wore buttoned panties. They went out with the horse and buggy."

"You see, Agnes, you don't even remember the panties we wore. They had buttons across the back, five of them in a row. So after I'd unbuttoned you I helped you up on the seat. That's when we first heard the hornets buzzing, close to the roof."

"And there I was, just a little bit of a thing and zzzz-zzzzzzz-zzz they all came right at me!"

"Actually, Agnes, you were quite large for your age. What's more the hornets didn't attack either of us, at first.

"We had studied hornets that year in second grade and my teacher had said that they never bothered anyone who didn't bother them first. So I kept perfectly calm. I said, 'Don't bother them, Agnes, and they won't bother you!'"

"But those nasty hornets were already bothered, Gertrude. And you wouldn't let me out of there. You held me down on the seat."

"Nonsense, Agnes. At the very first sting I prepared to leave as soon as possible. I helped you down off the seat and started to button your panties, but the way you were screaming and jumping up and down made it very difficult for me."

"Of course I was screaming. Of course I was jumping up and down. That's what you would have been doing too, if the hornets had been stinging you, Gertrude."

"They *were* stinging me, Agnes. As I re-marked earlier, each of us was stung several times that day."

"I was stung hundreds of times. And why did you have to button my panties anyway? Why didn't you just let me out of there?"

"And have you running around outside with
your panties hanging down? What would people
have thought of you, Agnes?"

"You didn't care what people thought of *me*, Gertrude. You were always hauling my blouse down and jerking my stockings up just so people would say, 'Isn't Gertrude wonderful the way she looks after Agnes? Gertrude is a real little mother!'"

"I am simply going to ignore what you just said, Agnes. I shall merely point out that when I saw that one hornet in your hair, I acted immediately. I opened the door and took your hand and we both went out."

"And the hornets followed me. They poured out in a black cloud and came zooming after me."

"They did not follow you, Agnes. I had shut the door on them. But of course you ran screaming up the path just the same and Aunt Hattie came running out and . . ."

" . . . and cut off my hair because the hornets were all tangled up in my curls and Aunt Hattie was afraid to get close to me. And Mama cried when we got home and she saw how I looked."

"Agnes, how did Aunt Hattie cut off your hair if she was afraid to get close to you?"

"Of course, I remember now, Gertrude. Aunt Hattie put on her heavy garden gloves and then she wasn't afraid to get close to me. So then she cut off my hair!"

"Now I'll tell you what really happened, Agnes. Aunt Hattie did put on her garden gloves and then she just grabbed the one hornet in your hair and killed it. She certainly did not cut off your hair."

"Yes, she did, Gertrude."

"No, she didn't, Agnes."

"She did *so!*"

"She did *not!*"

"She did *so!*"

"She did *not!*"

"She did *so!*"

"She did *not!*"